broken promise

By Eleanor Robins

SADDLEBACK
EDUCATIONAL PUBLISHING

CHOICES

Break All Rules

Broken Promise

Don't Get Caught

Double-Cross

Easy Pass

Friend or Foe?

No Exceptions

No Limits

Pay Back

Trust Me

SADDLEBACK
EDUCATIONAL PUBLISHING
www.sdlback.com

ISBN-13: 978-1-61651-591-1
ISBN-10: 1-61651-591-0
eBook: 978-1-61247-237-9

Printed in Malaysia

21 20 19 18 17   6 7 8 9 10

Meet the Characters from

broken promise

Josh:	dates Kate, has a driver's license and his own car, makes a choice
Josh's Dad:	asks Josh to keep his promise
Kate:	dates Josh, likes to go to dances, wants Josh to do the right thing
Cooper:	dates Nikki, is Josh's best friend
Nikki:	dates Cooper

chapter

1

Josh stood in his driveway. He was washing his car. His dad was helping him.

Josh sprayed some water on the car. He put the hose down. Then he picked up a cloth. Josh started to wipe the car with it. He asked his dad, "Do you know what next week is, Dad?"

His dad laughed. Then his dad said, "Yes, Josh. I know. It will be six months since you got your driver's license."

Josh said, "It's been a long six months. I can hardly wait for next week to get here. Then Kate can ride with me."

Kate was his girlfriend. They had been dating for four months.

Right now only a member of Josh's family could ride with him. Kate couldn't ride with him. And they had to ride with someone else when they went out.

His dad said, "Next week one of your friends can ride with you. But only one friend. Don't forget that, Josh. You can't have more than one friend ride with you."

"I know, Dad," Josh said.

All of Josh's friends were under 21. And only one friend under 21 could ride with him at a time. That was the law.

"Don't forget that, Josh," his dad said.

"I won't," Josh said.

"Don't let more than one friend ride with you at a time. Or you'll take a big chance. The police might stop you. Then you'll be in big trouble," his dad said.

"I know," Josh said.

"And that's not all. The police might not see you. But you know how people talk," his dad said.

Josh knew that was true. People liked to talk. They liked to tell what they knew about other people.

His dad said, "Don't let more than one friend ride in your car. Someone might tell me. Then you'll be in big trouble with me."

Josh knew what that meant.

His dad would take his car away from him. Josh wouldn't get to drive it. It would be a long time before he got his car back.

For a few more minutes Josh and his dad washed the car. They didn't talk. Then his dad said, "You'll still have to be home before midnight. Don't forget that, Josh."

"I won't," Josh said.

That was part of the law. Drivers his age couldn't drive between midnight and 6 a.m. Josh and his dad washed the car a while longer.

Then his dad said, "You know you can't double date. And you know your friend, Cooper, will want to double date with you."

Cooper was Josh's best friend. And Cooper did want to double date with him. Cooper had already talked to Josh about it. But Josh had told him that they couldn't double date.

"Yes, Dad. I know. I told Cooper we can't double date," Josh said. Josh and his dad didn't talk for a few minutes.

Then his dad said, "I want you to promise me something, Josh."

"What?" Josh asked. But he was sure

he knew what his dad wanted him to promise.

"Promise me that you'll only have one friend in your car at a time," his dad said.

"I promise," Josh said. And Josh meant it.

His dad said, "Don't break your promise to me, Josh. Or you know what will happen. I'll take your car away from you. You know I'll do it. And it will be a long time before you drive your car again."

"Yes, Dad. I know," Josh said.

Josh didn't have any doubts about it.

chapter 2

It was the next Monday. Josh was at home. His teachers had a meeting. So Josh had a day off from school. His dad had a day off, too.

Josh said, "I thought this day would never come. I've had my driver's license for six months. Now Kate can ride with me. I can hardly wait to take her for a ride."

His dad said, "Don't forget, Josh. Only one friend can ride with you at a time."

"I know. I won't forget," Josh said.

"Just don't forget you made a promise to me, Josh," his dad said.

"I won't forget, Dad," Josh said. He knew he had made a promise. And he would keep it.

"Is it okay for me to go over to see Kate now? I'd like to take her for a ride." Josh said.

His dad said, "Yes, Josh. But don't stay out too long. You promised you would help me with some yard work."

"I know I did, Dad. I won't be gone long," Josh said. Josh hurried outside, and got in his car.

Before starting the engine he sent Kate a text message: "RU home? Do u know what today is?"

Kate called him back right away.

Josh said, "Do you know what today is?"

But he knew Kate already knew.

Kate said, "You know that I do. You've had your driver's license for six months today. Now I can ride with you. And we won't have to ride with someone else when we go out."

Josh said, "Yeah. And I won't have to worry about finding someone to drive us places."

It had been hard to find someone to drive them places. Most of his friends were his age. And they couldn't let a friend drive them.

Josh asked, "Kate, do you want to go for a ride now?"

"Oh, yes, Josh. Can you come and get me right now?" Kate asked.

Josh said, "Yeah. I'll be over there in a few minutes. But I wanted to speak to you first. Just to make sure that you were home."

"I'm home. And I can hardly wait to

ride with you," Kate said.

"I'll be there in a few minutes," Josh said. Josh hung up. His phone chirped. Josh had a new text message from Cooper: "Been 6 months. Take me for a ride."

Josh texted back: "Can't."

Cooper texted: "Why?"

"Taking Kate." Josh texted back.

Cooper texted: "Then when?"

Josh wrote back: "Don't know. Later. Need 2 help Dad."

Cooper wrote: "K. Call me."

Josh said: "K."

Cooper wrote: "I'll be glad when I can drive Nikki. "

Nikki was Cooper's girlfriend.

Josh texted: "Not 2 much longer."

Cooper answered: "2 months is 2 long."

Josh wrote: "GTG. Can't text and drive. Call u later."

Cooper texted: "K."

Josh started his car. He could hardly wait to get to Kate's house. Josh would take her for a ride.

chapter 3

It was ten minutes later. Josh stopped his car next to the curb in front of Kate's house.

Kate stood in the front yard. She ran over to Josh's car. She quickly opened the door on her side of the car. Then she got in.

She had a big smile on her face. She said, "This is great, Josh. Now I can ride with you."

"Yeah. I know," Josh said. Josh had a big smile on his face, too.

"Am I the first person to ride with you today? Or did you take Cooper for a drive first?" Kate asked.

"You are the first person, Kate. Cooper texted after I talked to you. But I told him he would have to wait until later," Josh said.

"Thanks for taking me for a ride first, Josh," Kate said.

"You knew I would," Josh said.

"I knew you had better take me for a ride first," Kate said. Then she laughed.

Josh laughed, too. Then he said, "Fasten your seat belt, Kate."

"Okay," Kate said. She quickly buckled her belt. Then Josh pulled away from the curb. And he started to drive down the street.

"Where do you want to go?" he asked.

"I don't care. We can go somewhere. Or we can just drive around. Whatever you want to do," Kate said.

"Let's just drive around. That way more people might see us," Josh said.

"I'm all for that. I like to be seen with you," Kate said.

That made Josh smile. They drove around for a few minutes. Then Kate said, "I can hardly wait until Friday night."

"Why?" Josh asked.

Kate said, "You know why. Our school dance is Friday night."

"I forgot about the dance," Josh said.

"How could you forget about it?" Kate asked.

She sounded surprised that Josh had forgotten.

"All I could think about was that my six months were almost up. And I couldn't think about anything else," Josh said.

"Then I guess it's okay you forgot about the dance," Kate said.

Josh wanted to tease Kate. So he said, "You do want to go to the dance with me? Don't you, Kate?" But he knew Kate did.

"You know I do. And you had better want to go with me," Kate said.

Josh smiled at Kate. Kate smiled back. Josh knew he needed to keep his eyes on the road. So he turned and looked at the road.

Kate said, "We can go to the dance in your car now. We don't have to ride with someone else. That's so great."

"Yeah. That will be great. We can go when we want and we can leave when we want to leave," Josh said.

"I'd like to go early to this dance," Kate said.

"Yeah. I know," Josh said.

They had gone late to the last dance.

Josh said, "I wish Cooper could drive Nikki to the dance. It's too bad they can't go with us."

"But you know he can't," Kate said.

"Yeah. I know," Josh said.

Josh knew how hard it was to get a ride. A few times it took him a long time to find someone over 21 to drive them. And a few times he couldn't find a ride for Kate and him. Josh hoped Cooper could get a ride to the dance.

chapter

4

It was later that same day. Josh had finished the yard work. And now he wanted to take Cooper for a ride.

Josh asked, "Do you have something else for me to do, Dad?"

"No, Josh. You've done all of the things I wanted you to do. So you don't have to help me any longer," his dad said.

"Cooper wants me to take him for a ride. Is it okay to do that now?" Josh asked.

"Yes. But don't stay out too long. Make

sure you're back in time for dinner," his dad said.

"I will be," Josh said.

Josh called Cooper on his cell phone. Cooper answered on the first ring. Josh asked, "Where are you?"

"At home," Cooper said.

"Do you have time to go for a ride now?" Josh asked.

"You bet. Can you come now?" Cooper asked.

"Yeah. I'll be over there in a few minutes. See you then," Josh said.

Josh quickly got off his cell phone. Then he hurried to his car. Josh wanted to get to Cooper's house. But Josh made sure he drove within the speed limit.

It wasn't long until Josh got to Cooper's house. Cooper hurried over to Josh's car. He quickly climbed in and sat on the front seat.

"This is great, Josh," said Cooper. "Now the two of us can drive around together."

"Where do you want to go?" Josh asked.

"For now let's just drive around. So people can see us," Cooper said.

"Okay," Josh said. The two boys drove around for a few minutes.

Then Cooper asked, "Are you and Kate going to the dance on Friday night?"

"Yeah. Are you and Nikki going?" Josh asked. Josh was sure they were.

"I hope so. But I don't know yet," Cooper said.

That surprised Josh. "Why don't you know? Nikki wants to go with you. Doesn't she? The two of you didn't have a fight. Did you?" Josh asked.

Cooper and Nikki never got mad at each other. So Josh didn't think they had a fight.

Cooper said, "No, Josh. We didn't have a fight. Nikki wants to go with me. But we have a problem."

"What?" Josh asked. But Josh was sure he knew what the problem was.

"I don't have a ride to get us to the dance. I hoped we could go with Greg," Cooper said.

Greg was Cooper's older brother.

"Did you ask Greg to take you?" Josh asked.

"Yeah. And he said he would. But his girlfriend has to go out of town. Her car is broken. So now he's driving her," Cooper said.

"Too bad," Josh said.

Josh wished he could take Cooper and Nikki. But he knew he couldn't do that. The boys drove around for a few minutes. They didn't talk.

Then Cooper looked over at Josh. He

asked, "What about you, Josh? Will you take us?"

Cooper knew Josh couldn't drive more than one friend at a time. So Josh was surprised Cooper asked him to do that.

Josh said, "You know I can't do that, Cooper. You know I can have only one friend in the car with me right now."

"Yeah. I know. But who would know you did?" Cooper asked.

"The police might see us. And they might stop me," Josh said.

"If you obey the speed limit. Stop at all of the stop signs and red lights. Then the police won't stop you. So you won't get into trouble," Cooper said.

"Maybe. But I don't want to take that chance," Josh said.

"Take us, Josh, please," Cooper said.

"I want to take you. But I can't. I don't want to take a chance that the police might stop me. And I made a promise to my dad," Josh said.

"What kind of promise?" Cooper asked.

"I said I wouldn't have more than one friend in the car with me. And I meant it. I won't go back on my promise to my dad," Josh said.

"How would your dad know that you took us?" Cooper asked.

Josh didn't answer.

"Come on, Josh. Take us. You're my best friend," Cooper said.

"I know I am. But I can't do it. You ask around. And I'll ask around. Maybe we can find someone else to take you. But I can't," Josh said.

Cooper was his best friend. And Josh wanted to help him. But he had to do what was right. He couldn't take Cooper and Nikki to the dance.

chapter 5

It was the night before the dance. Josh was talking to Kate about it.

Kate said, "I can hardly wait. The band should be great. And we'll have a lot of fun."

"Yeah. I know," Josh said. But Josh knew he didn't sound as if he thought they would.

"You don't sound like you think the dance will be fun. Don't you want to go, Josh?" Kate asked.

"Sure. I want to go. But I was thinking

about Cooper and Nikki," Josh said.

"Why were you thinking about them?" Kate asked. She sounded surprised.

"I talked to Cooper a little while ago. He still hasn't found anyone to take them to the dance. So he isn't sure that he and Nikki will be able to go. I feel bad about it," Josh said.

"So do I. But it isn't too late. Maybe Cooper will still find someone to take them," Kate said.

Josh asked, "But who? I think Cooper has asked every guy in the school who has a car. But no one can drive more than one friend at a time."

Kate said, "Maybe something will work out. I sure hope so. I know how much Nikki wants to go to the dance."

"I wish I could do something," Josh said.

"But there isn't anything you can do.

You know they can't go with us," Kate said.

"I know. But Cooper is my best friend. And I wish I could take them," Josh said.

"But you can't, Josh. So don't worry about it," Kate said.

"I feel bad about it. Cooper asked me to take them," Josh said.

"He did what?" Kate asked. She sounded surprised.

"He asked me to take them. I had to tell him that I can't do it," Josh said.

"But he knows that you can get into trouble if you take more than one friend. It wasn't fair of him to ask you that," Kate said.

"Cooper thinks I can take them and not get into trouble. Maybe he's right. Maybe I should take them," Josh said.

"Don't even think about doing that, Josh," Kate said. She sounded mad.

"The police might stop you. And then you would lose your license. Cooper knows that, Josh," Kate said.

"He said if I obey the speed limit and don't do anything wrong, the police won't stop me," Josh said.

"It's still wrong, Josh. And you know that," Kate said.

"Yeah. I know. But Cooper is my best friend," he said again.

"Maybe the police wouldn't stop you. But your dad might find out. Then he would take your car away from you," Kate said.

"Yeah. I know. But maybe he wouldn't find out," Josh said.

"Maybe not. But you know how people talk," Kate said.

"Yeah. I do," Josh said.

Josh knew he shouldn't take Cooper and Nikki to the dance. But Cooper was his best friend. And Josh knew how he would feel if he couldn't go with Kate. Josh was sure that Cooper would feel the same way about Nikki.

Josh knew what he should do. But he wasn't sure that was what he would end up doing.

chapter

6

It was the day of the dance. School was over for the day. Josh was at home. He stood in his driveway. And he was washing his car.

Josh's cell phone rang. He dried his hands on a towel. And then he answered the phone.

Cooper said, "Yo, it's me. What're you doing?"

"Washing my car," Josh said.

"You sure do wash your car a lot," Cooper said.

"Yeah. I know. But I want it to look nice," Josh said.

"Why do you wash it so much? A little dirt won't hurt it," Cooper said.

"Yeah. I know. But I want it to look good tonight," Josh said.

"The dance doesn't start until after it gets dark. So why wash it? Who would see any dirt on it in the dark?" Cooper asked.

"That doesn't matter. I still want it to be clean for the dance," Josh said.

"Don't wash it too much. You don't want to wash the paint off," Cooper said.

Josh thought Cooper was joking. But Josh wasn't sure he was. The boys talked about school for a few minutes.

Then Cooper said, "I bet you and Kate will have fun tonight. I heard the band is great."

"Yeah. That's what I heard, too," Josh said.

"I sure wish Nikki and I could go. I know we would have a great time," Cooper said.

"You didn't find anyone to take you to the dance? I thought you were going to ask a guy that Greg knows," Josh said.

"I asked him. But he's taking another couple," Cooper said.

"Too bad," Josh said.

Josh felt bad for Cooper. He wished he could take Cooper and Nikki to the dance.

Josh said, "There are a few hours before the dance, Cooper. Maybe you can still find someone to take you."

"No way. There isn't anyone else to ask. You have to take Nikki and me tonight, Josh. You just have to take us. Or else we can't go," Cooper said.

"I'm sorry, Cooper. But you know I can't do that," Josh said.

"Doesn't it mean anything to you that I'm your best friend? Best friends help each other, don't they?" Cooper asked.

"Yes, they do. But I still can't take you, Cooper," Josh said.

"I thought I was your best friend. But maybe you don't feel that way about me. I need help tonight. And friends help each other," Cooper said.

Josh knew Cooper was right. Friends did help each other. Cooper had helped Josh a lot of times.

"Okay, Cooper. I know I shouldn't do it. But I'll take you and Nikki," Josh said.

"You will?" Cooper asked. He sounded very surprised.

"Yeah. I will. But don't tell anyone that I am doing it," Josh said.

"I won't. I'll tell Nikki not to tell anyone. This means a lot to me, Josh.

You're a great friend. And a great guy," Cooper said.

But Josh didn't feel like a great guy. He knew what he said he would do was wrong. But the dance should be a lot of fun. And he couldn't let Cooper and Nikki miss it.

Josh wished he hadn't made that promise to his dad. He wasn't going to keep the promise. Josh felt very bad about that.

chapter 7

It was Friday night. Josh was at Kate's house. He sat in her living room. Kate and her mom were there, too.

Kate's mom said, "Don't forget, Kate. You have to be home before midnight."

"I know, Mom. I won't forget. I'll be home before then," Kate said.

Her mom said, "Have fun at the dance."

"We will," Josh and Kate both said at the same time. Josh and Kate hurried outside to Josh's car.

Kate said, "I can hardly wait to get to the dance. We'll have so much fun."

Josh opened the car door for Kate. He made sure she got in the car okay. Then he hurried to his side of the car. He got in.

Kate said, "This will be a great night, Josh. I'm sure of it."

"Yeah. It will be. I'm sure of it, too," Josh said.

But Josh wasn't sure it would be. He knew he shouldn't drive Cooper and Nikki to the dance. And Josh was very worried about it.

Josh started the car. He drove for a few minutes. He and Kate didn't talk. Then Josh turned right to go to Cooper's house.

Kate said, "Why did you turn right, Josh? The dance is the other way."

Josh said, "I know. But I told Cooper I would drive Nikki and him to the dance."

"You told Cooper what?" Kate yelled.

"Cooper couldn't find anyone to take them to the dance. So he asked me to take them. And I said I would," Josh said.

"I can't believe you told Cooper that. You know you can't drive them to the dance. Just think of the trouble you can get into," Kate said.

"I know. But Cooper is my best friend," Josh said.

"A real friend wouldn't ask you to do that. So Cooper isn't much of a friend. He knows the trouble you could get into," Kate said. She sounded very mad.

Josh knew Kate would be mad. But he didn't think she would be *that* mad.

"You aren't being fair, Kate. Cooper just wants to go to the dance with Nikki. Just like I want to go with you," Josh said.

Kate said, "I'll say it again, Josh. A real friend wouldn't ask you to do that.

So Cooper isn't much of a friend."

"Why are you so mad at Cooper? I'm the one who might get into trouble. Not you," Josh said.

Kate said, "But I care about you, Josh. And I don't want you to get into trouble. I don't want you to lose your license. Or for your dad to take your car away."

Josh said, "Don't be mad, Kate. I know you're right. I shouldn't have said that I would drive Cooper and Nikki to the dance. But it's too late now. I have to drive them."

Kate was mad at him. Josh knew he would worry all night about it. And he knew that he would worry that he might get into trouble with the police or his dad.

Josh didn't think the dance would be much fun now. He was going to break a promise to his dad. So maybe the dance wouldn't be fun for him.

chapter 8

Josh and his dad sat in the living room. He asked, "How was the dance, Josh?"

"I had a great time," Josh said.

But that wasn't true. Josh had spent most of the night worried that he would get into trouble with the police or his dad. Then his dad's cell phone rang.

His dad went into another room to answer it.

A few minutes later, his dad came back into the living room. He looked very mad.

Josh was sure someone had told his dad. His dad said, "You made me a promise, Josh. I thought I could trust you."

Josh didn't say anything. His dad said, "Did you think I wouldn't find out, Josh?"

"About what?" Josh asked. But Josh was sure he knew what his dad meant.

"You drove your friend and his girlfriend to the dance last night, didn't you?" his dad said.

"Yes," Josh said.

"And you know only one friend can ride with you at a time," his dad said.

"Yes, I know that," Josh said.

"What do you have to say for yourself?" his dad asked. He looked very mad.

Josh said, "Cooper is my best friend. He couldn't find anyone else to drive them to the dance. And they needed a ride. So I took them."

He wanted to help his friend. But Josh knew that wasn't the way to do it. Why didn't he try to think of another way to help Cooper?

His dad said, "I told you people talk, Josh. I told you that someone might tell me."

"I know, Dad. But Cooper is my best friend. And friends help each other," Josh said.

"Not when one friend has to get into trouble to do it. And you knew you might get into trouble with the police. Did you forget about that?" his dad asked.

"No. But I didn't give the police a reason to stop me. I made sure of that. I didn't speed. I stopped at every stop sign and red light," Josh said.

His dad said, "I'm glad. But you knew you could still get into trouble with me.

But I guess you thought I wouldn't find out about it."

Josh didn't say anything. What could he say?

"You promised me, Josh. I thought I could trust you. But I was wrong," his dad said.

"I'm sorry, Dad," Josh said. And he was sorry. Josh felt very bad that he had broken his promise to his dad.

His dad said, "I'm sure you're sorry, Josh. I hope it's because you feel bad about what you did. And not because I found out."

Josh said, "I felt sorry last night. But it was too late. I had already promised Cooper that I would drive him."

"And you thought it was okay to break your promise to me. But it wasn't okay to break your promise to your friend," his dad said.

"I was wrong, Dad. And I'm sorry. I didn't want to break my promise to you," Josh said.

Josh's dad held out his hand. He said, "Give me your car keys, Josh. It will be a long time before you get to drive your car again."

Josh pulled his car keys out of his pocket. He gave the keys to his dad. How long would it be before he got to drive again? Josh knew he couldn't ask his dad when that time might come.

But he was sure it would be a long time.

consider this...

1. What would you do if you had to choose between helping someone and keeping a promise to another person?

2. Why is it a bad idea to talk about other people?

3. What does Cooper's request tell us about how he feels about Josh?

4. How might Josh have avoided breaking his promise? What else could he have done to help Cooper and Nikki?

5. What is the lesson Josh's dad wants to teach when he says: "Not when one friend has to get into trouble to do it."?